WHO'S NEXT DOOR?

Written by Mayuko Kishira

Illustrated by Jun Takabatake

Deep in the woods, there are two houses.
Chicken lives in the house with the red roof.

No one lives in the house with the blue roof.

Chicken wakes up every morning at sunrise.
He eats breakfast and reads the paper.
He eats lunch and takes a nap.

He eats a snack and goes for a walk.
He eats dinner and gets ready for bed.
By sundown, Chicken is sound asleep.

One morning, Chicken steps outside—
and what a surprise!
It looks like someone has moved in next door.

Chicken is happy.
He enjoys living on his own,
but sometimes he feels lonely.

"Is he still sleeping? Maybe he's out."

All day long, Chicken paces back and forth
in front of the house with the blue roof.
But no one comes out.
Finally, it's time to go to bed.
"I'm sure I'll get to meet my neighbor tomorrow."

But the next day,
the following day,
and the day after that,
Chicken didn't meet his neighbor.

"Shouldn't he come to my house to say hello?"

"Maybe he's tired from moving."

"I like being alone, anyway."

"But it would be so much fun to have a friend."

"I just *have* to meet my neighbor!"

Chicken decides to write a letter
and leave it on his neighbor's door.

That night, the door of the house with the blue roof opens.
Someone comes out.

It's Owl.
Owl is the opposite of Chicken.

That's right.
Every night since he moved in, Owl has been going
to the house with the red roof to say hello.
But, by then, Chicken is already asleep.

Owl is overjoyed to find the letter.

The next morning, Chicken wakes up.
He finds an answer to his letter and is also overjoyed.

Chicken gets ready.

He prepares some food.

He decorates his house.

And then he waits.

He waits...

and waits...
and waits...
and waits.

That evening, Owl is so excited that he's already up
and waiting before it gets dark.

He waits...
and waits...
and waits.

"Is it too late for him to come over?
I'll check outside to make sure."

"Is it too early to visit?
I'll step outside to make sure."

The two doors open.

"Hello!"

"Hello!"

Deep in the woods, there are two houses.
Chicken lives in the house with the red roof.
Owl lives in the house with the blue roof.

Look!
There's something between the two houses.
What could it be?

Chicken and Owl don't get to see each other very often,
but they talk to each other all the time!

Text © 2011 Mayuko Kishira
Illustrations © 2011 Jun Takabatake
Translation © Shana Rieko Shimizu/KAN Communications Inc.

Published in North America in 2014 by Owlkids Books Inc.

Published in Japan under the title *Otonari-san* in 2011 by BL Publishing Co., Ltd., Kobe.

English translation rights arranged with BL Publishing Co., Ltd., Kobe, through Japan Foreign-Rights Centre

Owlkids Books acknowledges the financial support of the Canada Council for the Arts, the Ontario Arts Council, the Government of Canada through the Canada Book Fund (CBF) and the Government of Ontario through the Ontario Media Development Corporation's Book Initiative for our publishing activities.

Published in Canada by
Owlkids Books Inc.
10 Lower Spadina Avenue
Toronto, ON M5V 2Z2

Published in the United States by
Owlkids Books Inc.
1700 Fourth Street
Berkeley, CA 94710

Kishira, Mayuko [Otonari-san. English]
    Who's next door / written by Mayuko Kishira ; illustrated by Jun Takabatake.

Translation of: Otonari-san. Translation by: Shana Rieko Shimizu.

ISBN 978-1-77147-071-1 (bound)

    1. Chickens--Juvenile fiction. 2. Owls--Juvenile fiction. I. Takabatake, Jun, illustrator II. Shimizu, Shana Rieko, translator III. Title. IV. Title: Otonari-san. English.

PZ7.K64Wh 2014   j895.6'36   C2014-900087-1

Library of Congress Control Number: 2014931869

Manufactured in Dongguan, China, in April 2014, by Toppan Leefung Packaging & Printing (Dongguan) Co., Ltd. Job #BAYDC9

A   B   C   D   E   F

Owl kids Publisher of Chirp, chickaDEE and OWL
www.owlkidsbooks.com